Anthony Browne

# WILLY THE WIZARD

Alfred A. Knopf • New York

THIS IS A BORZOI BOOK PUBLISHED BY ALFRED A. KNOPF, INC.

Copyright © 1995 A.E.T. Browne & Partners
All rights reserved under International and Pan-American Copyright Conventions.
Published in the United States by Alfred A. Knopf, Inc., New York.
Distributed by Random House, Inc., New York.
First published in the United Kingdom in 1995 by Julia MacRae Books.

*Library of Congress Cataloging-in-Publication Data*
Browne, Anthony.
Willy the wizard / by Anthony Browne.
p.   cm.
Summary: Willy the chimpanzee loves to play soccer, but he is never picked for
a team until a stranger gives him some shoes that he is certain are magic.
ISBN: 0-679-87644-8 (trade) — ISBN: 0-679-97644-2 [library binding]
[1. Soccer—Fiction.   2. Chimpanzees—Fiction.]   I. Title.
PZ7.B81984W1   1995   95-137   [E]—dc20

ISBN: 0-679-87644-8 (trade)
0-679-97644-2 [library binding]

Manufactured in Singapore   10 9 8 7 6 5 4 3 2 1

*For Nicholas, Francesca, and Jacqueline*

Willy loved soccer. But there was a problem—
he didn't have any boots. He couldn't afford them.

Willy went eagerly to the practice sessions
every week. He ran and chased and tried to join
in, but no one passed the ball to him.
He was never picked for the team.

One evening, when Willy was walking home past the
old pie factory, he saw someone kicking a ball around.
The stranger was wearing old-fashioned soccer gear, like
the clothes Willy remembered his dad wearing.
But he was good. Very good.

Willy watched for a while, and when the ball came
over to him, he kicked it back. They played
silently together, passing the ball back and forth.

Then the stranger did something very odd.
He unlaced his boots, took them off, and without
saying a word, handed them to Willy.

Willy stared at them with wonder.

When he looked up,
no one was there.

Taking great care not to step
on any cracks in the pavement,
Willy carried the boots home.

He cleaned and polished
them until they looked new.

Then he went slowly upstairs,
counting *every* step (sixteen),
washed his hands and face *very* thoroughly,
brushed his teeth for *exactly* four minutes,
put on his pajamas (always the top first,
always with *four* buttons fastened),
used the toilet, and dived into bed.
(He had to be in bed before the
flushing stopped, for who knows what would
happen if he wasn't?)
Every morning, he repeated all these
actions in reverse. *Every* morning.

For the next soccer practice, Willy proudly took along his boots. But the other players weren't exactly impressed . . .

. . . until they saw him play.
Wearing the old boots, Willy was fantastic!

When the captain posted the
lineup for next Saturday's match,
Willy could hardly believe his eyes.

He was so pleased that he ran all the way home (being very careful not to step on the cracks).

Every day, Willy put on his boots and practiced
shooting, dribbling, passing, and heading.
He got better and better. Willy was sure
his boots were magic.

Every evening, Willy put on his boots and went
back to the old pie factory. There had been
something curiously familiar about the stranger
that made Willy want to see him again.
But he was never there.

On Friday night, Willy went through his
usual bedtime routine.
He went slowly upstairs counting *every* step
(still sixteen),
washed his hands and face *very* thoroughly,
brushed his teeth for *exactly* four minutes,
put on his pajamas (the top first, with
*four* buttons fastened),
used the toilet, and dived into bed
before the flushing stopped *(whew!)*.

But Willy was too excited to sleep.
Even when he drifted off, he spent an
uncomfortable night dreaming of disasters.

In the morning, he woke up with a start.
It was 9:45, and the match started at 10!
He leaped out of bed,
threw on his clothes,
raced down the stairs,
and dashed out the door.

Willy ran all the way to the soccer field.

When he got there, the other players were already
changed. The captain threw Willy his gear, and he
put it on. Then the awful thought struck him . . .
HE HAD FORGOTTEN HIS BOOTS!
Someone found him another pair.
"Y-you don't understand . . ." he said, but the
team had already gone onto the field.

The crowd's roar turned to laughter when Willy emerged from the locker room. Willy grinned, but inside he felt angry.

The game started. Willy was amazed how fast it
was. Within minutes, the opposition had scored.
1–0! From the restart the ball shot out to Willy on
the wing. He had no time to think. He just ran
with the ball at his feet.

Willy was magic—the ball seemed to be attached to
him by an invisible thread. He dribbled past three
opponents and sent in a perfect cross. GOAL!

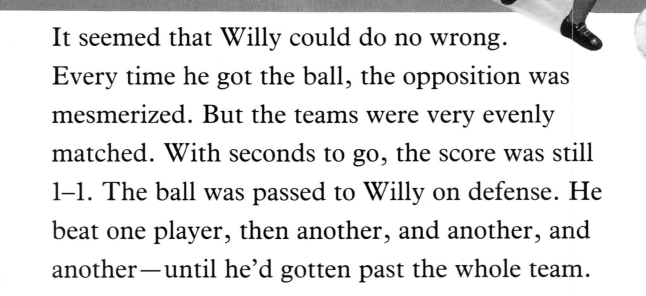

It seemed that Willy could do no wrong.
Every time he got the ball, the opposition was
mesmerized. But the teams were very evenly
matched. With seconds to go, the score was still
1–1. The ball was passed to Willy on defense. He
beat one player, then another, and another, and
another—until he'd gotten past the whole team.

Only the goalkeeper to beat! The keeper
was huge and the net looked tiny.
Could Willy do it?

He could! The crowd was spellbound as Willy
conjured up the perfect shot. GOALLLLL ! ! !

"WILLY THE WIZARD! WILLY THE WIZARD!"
chanted the crowd.

Later, on the way home,
Willy thought about the
boots and the stranger.
And he smiled.

3

| DATE DUE | | | |
|---|---|---|---|
| | | | |
| | | | |
| | | | |
| | | | |
| | | | |
| | | | |
| | | | |
| | | | |
| | | | |
| | | | |

BTSB  Bound to Stay Bound Books, Inc